The Jack Book

Who can help him on sunny days and on stormy days?

Written by Judy Wimberley

Illustrations by Sallie Dean

WestBow Press books may be ordered through booksellers or by contacting:

WestBow Press
A Division of Thomas Nelson
1663 Liberty Drive
Bloomington, IN 47403
www.westbowpress.com
1-(866) 928-1240

Because of the dynamic nature of the Internet, any web addresses or
links contained in this book may have changed since publication and may
no longer be valid. The views expressed in this work are solely those
of the author and do not necessarily reflect the views of the publisher,
and the publisher hereby disclaims any responsibility for them.

ISBN: 978-1-4497-8339-6 (sc)
ISBN: 978-1-4497-8340-2 (e)

Library of Congress Control Number: 2013901597

Printed in the United States of America

WestBow Press rev. date: 03/07/2013

WESTBOW
PRESS
A DIVISION OF THOMAS NELSON

Dedicated to

JACK

Emma!

Ellie

Caroline

Sara

Hank

Lauren

Keely

Luke

BOONE

Claire

←Grant

↖Addy

whom Grandma loves very, very much!

...and for all children everywhere,
all of whom are very precious gifts from God.
May this be read to them
by someone who loves them very, very much.

Jack is a little boy who loves to play with cars, balls, trains and in the sand. He is a very precious gift from God to his Daddy, Mommy, PaPa, BenBen, Grandma, GranGran and all his aunts and uncles and cousins and friends who love him very much.

Jack loves days when the sun is out, not hiding behind clouds. A sunny day he calls it.

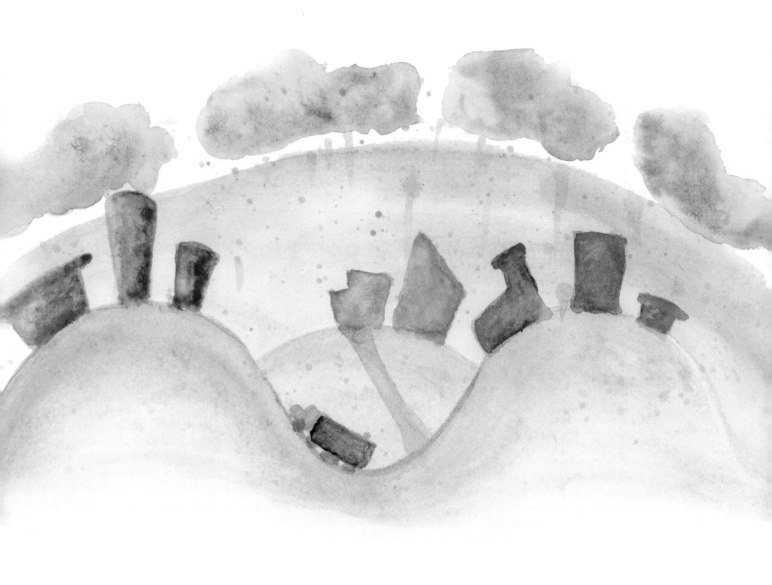

But some days are stormy days when clouds hide the sun and rain falls and wind blows and we see lightning and hear thunder. A blustery day as some would say.

On stormy days what would someone need to be safe?

On stormy days, if you were a ship, you would need an anchor.

On stormy days, if you were
a building, you would need a
strong foundation.

On stormy days, if you were a tree,
you would need deep roots.

On stormy days, if you were a baby
chick, you would need to be under
your mother's wing.

In the storm, Noah and the
animals needed an ark.

On stormy days, if you are a person, you need a rock that is higher than you are tall.

Sometimes as Jack grows up to be a big boy and a big man, he will have blustery days. Oh, not just days of rain and wind when you need an umbrella and coat, but days where there are storms of difficult things, problems, pain, things that hurt, confuse, and put a frown or an afraid look on your face.

What does Jack need for
those kind of stormy days?

An anchor

A strong
foundation

Deep roots

Protective wing

An ark

A rock that is
higher than he.

Jack needs someone who can promise to never leave him. Who can promise him that?

Can Mommy or Daddy or all the people who love him promise him that?

No, they cannot, but JESUS can because He is God.

JESUS can be Jack's anchor

Jack's strong foundation

Jack's deep roots

Jack's protective wing

Jack's ark

Jack's rock that is higher than he.

JESUS promises He is all of these.
JESUS can be Jack's safe place in all
the storms of his life.

Jack and you can
know JESUS when you
understand you have
done wrong things

and you understand
that Jesus died for
all the wrong things
you have done

and that He came back to life. Hooray!

Jack can ask JESUS to come into his life of sunny days

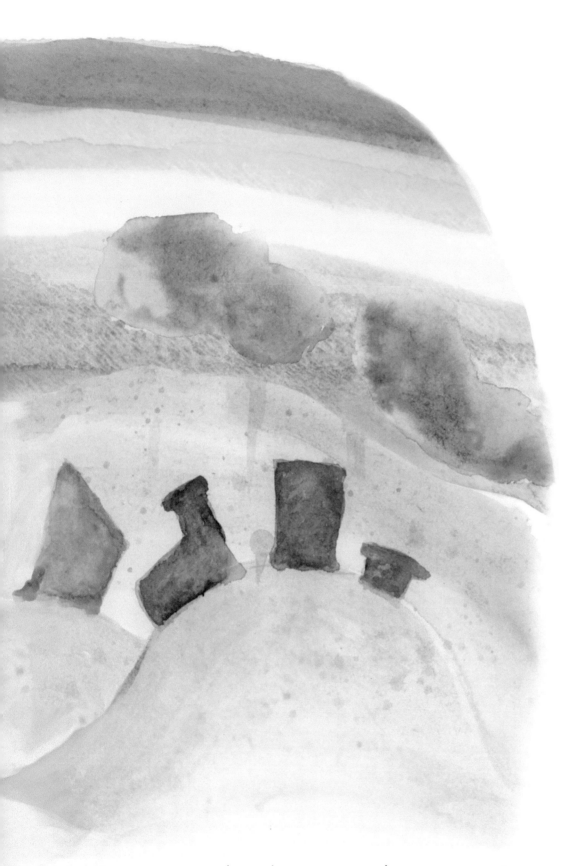

and stormy days.
JESUS can take care of Jack
in all of his days.

The Bible tells us how JESUS is our anchor, our foundation, our root, our protective wing, our ark, our rock that is higher than we are.

In the Bible, JESUS promises to never leave us nor forsake us.

As Jack grows up, he is learning many things. He is learning about sunny days and stormy days. Most importantly, he is learning about JESUS who loves him very, very much!

JESUS is the Promise Maker and
Promise Keeper Jack and you
need to live life on sunny days
and on stormy days.

JESUS is the one who will always
love Jack and always love you.

For ♡ to ♡ times:

♥ Reading this book at bedtime will help establish a habit to end the day remembering who Jesus is and how much He loves and cares for each child.

♥ As children become familiar with the book, start the phrase and let them fill it in, i.e., "if you were a tree, you would need _____ etc."

♥ Take time to talk about an anchor; look for pictures of them or even take time to go to a boat dock to see one. Talk about why a ship or boat needs an anchor. Help them see how Jesus being their anchor can help them on sunny days and stormy days.

♥ On walks, watch for deep roots. Try to pull them up. Talk about what roots do for a tree on sunny days and stormy days.

♥ When visiting a barn or egg farm watch for hens with chicks under their wings. Talk about how a baby chick feels under its mother's wing. Check online sources for videos of baby chicks under their mother's wing.

♥ Try to watch when a house foundation is being poured and talk about the importance of a foundation. Build some sand castles on the beach and watch how quickly they disappear because they don't have a strong foundation.

♥ Go rock climbing and talk about what a difference being high up on a rock means for sunny days and stormy days.

♥ Use the terminology of "sunny day" and "stormy day" for a heart check for children at bedtime. Was today a "sunny day" or a "stormy day" for you? What can we remember about Jesus that will help you remember that He is with you and is strong on both sunny days and stormy days?

♥ When children are in a situation of stormy days that are not of their own making, remind them of who loves them - Jesus who is their anchor, ark, strong foundation, etc. Then remind them of family members and friends who love them very much.

♥ Let meal time prayer be a time of praise to God for who He is by letting each one at the table thank God for one of the things He is, i.e., our deep roots, our ark, etc.

♥ When sad things happen and there are difficulties in life and in the world, read the Jack Book and ask, "What can we remember about God that will help us know He is with us in this sad or difficult time?"

♥ Guide children in learning to pray for others by asking God to specifically show who He is in someone's life. If a playmate is facing something hard, teach the child how to ask "God, please help Tammy in this sad time and help her know that You can be her anchor and keep her strong and steady each day."

♥ Have some creative times to let children draw pictures of themselves standing on a tall rock, or in an ark, or on a boat with a big anchor or under a mother hen's wing. Help them personalize the ways that Jesus loves them.

♥ As children learn to read, let them read the verses from the Bible that describe Jesus as being their anchor, strong foundation, deep root, etc. so that a child understands true information about Jesus comes from the scriptures. Using a family Bible would help a child begin to connect that scripture is true for adults as well as children.

Anchor: Hebrews 6:18b-19a

Strong Foundation: Matthew 7:24-27; Luke 6:47-48; Isaiah 28:16

Deep Roots: Ephesians 3:17; Colossians 2:7

Mother's Wing: Matthew 23:37b; Luke 13:34; Deuteronomy 32:10b-11

Ark: Genesis 6:17-18; 7:18; Hebrews 11:7

Rock: Psalm 27:5; Psalm 61:2-3; 1 Corinthians 10:4

♥ Talk about how rainbows are a reminder that God keeps his promises by reading the story of Noah (Gen.6:8-9:17 and the great reminder about God and His promise keeping in Deut. 7:9).

♥ Let them read the gospel message from the Bible so they can enter into a relationship with God the Father through the death, burial and resurrection of Jesus for the wrong things they have thought, said, and done.

    John 3:16

    1 Corinthians 15:3b-4

    Colossians 2:9

    John 1:12

♥ Be careful with what you promise children since you cannot always be in control of fulfilling promises. Be lavish with what you teach them about what Jesus promises because He can and will fulfill His promises.

♥ A great promise of Jesus that He made and will keep is Hebrews 13:5b. Teach them the verse by having them hold up one hand and say one word per finger:
"I will never leave you nor forsake you." (NKJV)

♥ Place this book in the hands of children who need to know that Jesus loves them very, very much. Better yet, read it to them.

CPSIA information can be obtained
at www.ICGtesting.com
Printed in the USA
BVIC010134110413
317795BV00006B

* 9 7 8 1 4 4 9 7 8 3 3 9 6 *